Khalil's Swagtown Adventure

W9-AVD-189

Reach Incorporated | Washington, DC

Shout Mouse Press

Reach Education, Inc. / Shout Mouse Press
Published by
Shout Mouse Press, Inc.
www.shoutmousepress.org

Copyright © 2014 Reach Education, Inc.
ISBN-13: 978-0692300800 (Shout Mouse Press, Inc.)
ISBN-10: 0692300805

All rights reserved. No part of this book may be reproduced or transmitted in any form or by any means, electronic or mechanical, including photocopying, recording, or by an information storage and retrieval system, without written permission from the publisher, excepting brief quotes used in reviews.

Dedicated to all the kids who feel alone
and want a happy family.

Khalil sits in his favorite spot: the closet.

It's the farthest place in the house from his parents' room.
His parents are always arguing.
It makes him feel unwanted, like they're not a real family.
When he gets sad, Khalil goes to this secret place where he
can get away from the fighting.

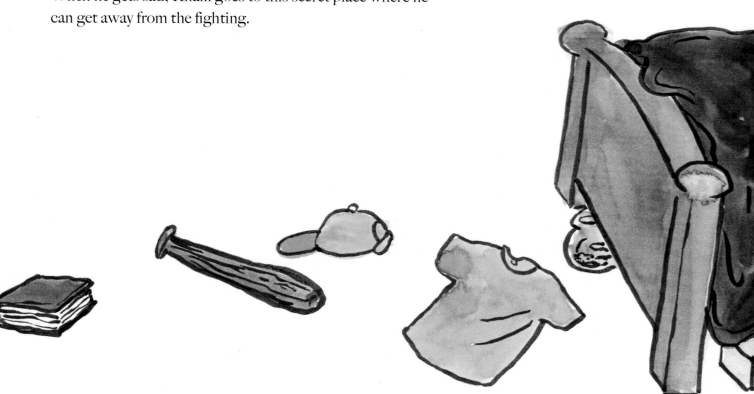

It's dark in the closet.

Outside, Khalil hears angry voices.
He tries to make himself into a ball.

He picks up a crayon and starts
writing a letter to himself.

Dear Khalil,
Mommy and daddy are arguing again. I wish there was somewhere I could go to get away.
From,
Khalil

"Khalil is the light in my sun
Without him I can't get anything done... ♪

He lays his head on his favorite Spiderman pillow and sings to himself. It's a song his mother used to sing to him when he was little.

Soon, he falls asleep.

A few hours later somebody taps him on the shoulder.

Khalil looks up, and sees his own face staring back at him. But the face is older.
"Who are you?" Khalil asks.
"Hi Khalil," says the stranger. "I'm Khalil! I'm the future you."
"Prove it," says Khalil.
"Ok," says the stranger. "You love Spiderman. Your favorite food is chili pizza. You've always wanted to go to Water World and ride the Hurricane, and you hate it when Mommy and Daddy fight."

Wow, you are me!" says Khalil.
"I know," says the future Khalil. "You can call me Bruh. I got your letter. I know just the place we should go."
"Ok," says Khalil.
"But first, we have to do a magic handshake to get there," Bruh tells him.

First they do a fist bump.
Then they wiggle their thumbs twice.
They dap each other up.
They bump hips.
And then they do the Nae Nae.

The Khalils feel the floor shaking. When they look down, a black circle appears beside them. They jump into it and slide down to a whole new world.

"Welcome to Swagtown," says Bruh.
They start bouncing when they land and can't stop because the ground is one giant trampoline. Across the road, there are purple broccoli trees. Bruh picks a piece of broccoli off the tree and tells Khalil to try it. Khalil eats it and starts smiling. "It tastes like candy corn!" he says.

Just then, a skinny guy with green fur walks up to them. He has a big head and six tiny feet.

"Khalil, this is my friend Flanty," says Bruh.
"Howdy!" says Flanty. "I'll be your tour guide."
"Wow," says Khalil. "You're so furry."
"You're so not-furry!" says Flanty, and they both laugh.
"Flanty, do you mind taking us to see the Bieberski family?" Bruh asks.
"Sure thing," says Flanty.

They jump from one trampoline to another like astronauts on the moon.

Next thing you know, they arrive at

the Bieberskis' house. It's a mansion
with rainbow walls. Khalil, Bruh, and
Flanty bounce up to the front door and
knock.

The door opens slowly, and a little girl
peeks out from behind. She has a
regular human body, but three eyes and
two different colored pigtails. On her
back are little fairy wings. She's wearing
a tutu, and she's smiling.

Khalil is a little afraid of her, but Bruh
pushes him forward.

"This is Markea Bieberski," says Bruh.
"Markea, this is Khalil."
"Nice to meet you," says Markea. "Do
you guys want to come in?"

Bruh and Khalil thank Flanty for taking them there.

"No problem," says Flanty, and bounces away.

The two boys go into the Bieberski mansion.

Inside, something smells really good.

"Is that what I think it is?" Khalil asks.

"It's chili pizza!" says Markea. "My dad made the pizza and my mom made the chili. I'm just about to get out some plates. Do you guys want some?"

Khalil's eyes glitter. "Swag! That's my favorite food!" He pumps his fist in the air.

They all go into the kitchen, where they see a man cooking and a lady washing the dishes. The woman looks just like Markea, but bigger, and the man has dreads instead of pigtails.

Mr. Bieberski shakes both of their hands, and Mrs. Bieberski gives them each a hug.

"We're just about to sit down to eat," says Mr. Bieberski. "Would you mind helping us set the table?"

After dinner, they all go to the living room and sit down to play charades. Khalil has to act out a monkey. He bends his knees, scratches his armpits, puffs his cheeks, and pulls out his ears. Markea's parents guess it right away.

"Wow!" says Khalil. "You guys are really good at this!"

"You have good acting skills," says Mrs. Bieberski with a smile.

Once they've gone through several rounds, Bruh says, "It's getting late, Khalil. We should probably get you home."

"Thanks for the food, Mr. and Mrs. B," says Khalil.
"You're very welcome, Khalil!" says Mr. B.
"Come back soon!" says Markea.

Khalil and Bruh do their magic handshake, and a black hole opens in the floor.

They wave goodbye to the Bieberskis and jump in. When they open their eyes, they're back in Khalil's closet.

Outside the door, Khalil's parents are yelling, just like they were when he left. He hears his mother scream: "You said YOU would do it!" He feels sadder than ever.

"My family never eats dinner together," he tells Bruh. "We never play charades. Markea's parents are like a team, and mine aren't. They just argue all the time, about everything."

"Write me a letter tomorrow like you did today, and I'll come back," says Bruh.

Then, suddenly, Bruh is gone.

The next day, Khalil wakes up to the smell of bacon.

He walks downstairs to the kitchen.

Khalil's father is sitting at the counter, eating bacon.
"Is there any more food, Daddy?" Khalil asks.
"I thought your mother was going to make you breakfast," his dad says, shrugging.

Khalil hears his mother talking on the phone in the next room.
He hears the words "money," "project," and "meeting." She's talking quickly.

She gets off the phone and walks into the kitchen. She smiles at Khalil, but stops smiling when she looks at his father.

"Is there more bacon?" she asks.
"No, Dad just made himself bacon," says Khalil.
"I didn't know you were hungry," says his father.
"You were supposed to make Khalil breakfast!" his mother says, angrily. "I have a meeting."
"Well look at you, Ms. I-Have-A-Job-And-I'm-So-Sassy," says his father. "I have things to do, too. I have to research job openings."
"It's about time," says his mother.

They start to yell at each other. Again.

Khalil doesn't feel hungry anymore.

He sprints up the stairs and heads right for his favorite spot, with a piece of paper and a crayon in his hand.

In the closet, he writes a letter:

Dear Bruh,
I don't feel so good.
Can you take me to
Swagtown so we
can hang out with
the Beiberskis?
From,
Khalil

Khalil puts the crayon down, and when he turns around, Bruh is smiling back at him from between a hoodie and a jacket.

"You ready to go?" Bruh asks.

They do their handshake, and once again, a black hole appears in the floor and they jump in.

Bruh and Khalil land on the trampoline street where they first arrived in Swagtown.

They see a familiar green furry figure bouncing towards them.

"Look, it's Flanty!" says Khalil.
"Howdy!" says Flanty. "What brings you back to Swagtown?"
"My mommy and my daddy are fighting again," says Khalil.
"You know," Flanty says, "the Bieberskis fight a lot, too. But they come together and talk about their problems and straighten things out."

They bounce over to the Bieberski mansion.
"Thanks for everything, Flanty," Bruh and Khalil say at the same time.
"No problem," says Flanty, saluting them as he bounces away.

Markea answers the door.

"Come on in, guys. But I'm sorry, my parents are having an argument," she says.

They come inside. Khalil feels a little scared. He doesn't want to be in the middle of a fight again so soon. He's expecting to hear yelling, but instead, he hears a conversation. The Bieberskis are sitting across from each other in the living room, talking.

"I thought you were going to feed the unicorns this morning," Mrs. B. says to Mr. B. "I fed them last night," says Mr. B. "It's your turn."

Khalil's hands tense up like they always do when his parents fight.

But then, Mrs. B. says, "I'm sorry, I was at work. It might have been my turn and I forgot."
"It's okay. It might have been my turn, too," says Mr. B. "Let's feed them together. And we can write out a schedule so we always know whose turn it is."
"Good idea, Sugarpea," says Mrs. B. "Let's go get the candy to feed them."

Khalil snaps his fingers. Suddenly, he has a great idea.
"Sorry, Markea. I have to go now. I have to get back to my family. I'll be back soon," he says.
"Okay, I understand," says Markea.

Bruh and Khalil do their handshake.

The hole in the floor opens, and just like that, they're back in the closet.

Khalil runs out of the closet and downstairs to the kitchen, grabbing his Spiderman pillow on the way to make himself feel more confident. His mom and dad are still there, and his mom's face is red, like she's about to cry. His dad looks like he's about to say something but holding himself back.

Khalil says, "Mommy, Daddy," but they don't look at him.

He throws the Spiderman pillow across the room.

They look at him and realize how upset he is, because normally he would never do that to his pillow.

"I'm tired of you arguing. We never do anything as a family. You guys don't act like parents because you're fighting all the time."

His dad looks at his feet, and his mom looks at the ceiling.

Khalil's dad clears his throat and says, "I'm sorry, I didn't realize that our fighting hurt you."

Khalil's dad looks over at his mom. She says, "You're right. Let's start over today. We need to do better for this family."

"Yes we do," Khalil's dad says. "And we will."
He puts his arm behind Khalil's mom's back. "We're sorry, Khalil."

"It's OK," says Khalil. "I know you don't mean to. And I have an idea. You guys are always fighting about who's supposed to make breakfast. How about we just do it together now?" Khalil suggests. "And then later we can make a schedule so everybody knows when it's their turn."

"That's a good idea, " Khalil's mom says. "I'll call and postpone my meeting."

"I guess I can put in that mechanic application later today," Khalil's dad says. "So what do you want for breakfast?"

Khalil thinks for a second. "Gummyworm pancakes!" he says.

Khalil's mom makes the batter, Khalil pours the batter into the pan, and Khalil's dad flips the pancakes.

It is scrumdiddlyumptious!

While they eat, Khalil's mom says, "I heard that on Saturday there's a family discount at Water World."

Khalil's dad says to Khalil, "Great, I can take you on your favorite ride, the Hurricane."

"For realzies? Can we all go together? I can't remember the last time we all went somewhere!"

Khalil's mom says, "Yeah! I want to go on the Hurricane, too."

As his mom and dad do the dishes, his mom
softly sings:

> Khalil is the light in the sun
> Without him I can't get anything done
> Khalil is the glaze in my box of donuts
> Without him, I would be a squirrel with no nuts
> I love love love my Khilly-Kim
> and I would not let anything
> happen to him!

That night before going to bed, Khalil writes one last letter:

Dear Bruh,
Things are better here. I don't need to go back to Swagtown right now because I like my actual home. But tell the Beiberskis hello and thank you! And thank YOU for your help too. See you in the future!
From,
Khalil

The End